## A stranger in the castle . . .

"Pretend you live in the Enchanted Castle. Where would you have your bedroom?" I asked.

"In the highest tower," Jessica said.

I studied the castle's windows, trying to decide which room would make the best bedroom.

"Look!" I said with a gasp. I pointed to one of the lower windows. "A man is looking out the window!"

"I don't see anything," Jessica said.

"He was right there!" I insisted.

"You're imagining things," Jessica said.

But I felt a shiver run up my spine. Something mysterious was going on in the Enchanted Castle. I was sure of it!

# Bantam Books in the SWEET VALLEY KIDS series

## SWEET VALLEY KIDS SUPER SNOOPER EDITIONS

## SWEET VALLEY KIDS SUPER SPECIAL EDITIONS

## SWEET VALLEY KIDS HAIR RAISER EDITIONS

SWEET VALLEY KIDS

# THE
# SECRET OF
# FANTASY FOREST

Written by
**Molly Mia Stewart**

Created by
**FRANCINE PASCAL**

Illustrated by
**Ying-Hwa Hu**

BANTAM BOOKS
NEW YORK • TORONTO • LONDON • SYDNEY • AUCKLAND

# To Mary Ann Boulton

## RL 2, 005-008

THE SECRET OF FANTASY FOREST

*A Bantam Book / October 1996*

*Sweet Valley High® and Sweet Valley Kids® are
registered trademarks of Francine Pascal.*

*Conceived by Francine Pascal.*

*Produced by Daniel Weiss Associates, Inc.
33 West 17th Street
New York, NY 10011.*

*Cover art by Susan Tang.*

ISBN: 0-553-48332-3

*Published simultaneously in the United States and Canada*

*Bantam Books are published by Bantam Books, a division of Bantam
Doubleday Dell Publishing Group, Inc. Its trademark, consisting of the
words "Bantam Books" and the portrayal of a rooster, is Registered in the
U.S. Patent and Trademark Office and in other countries. Marca
Registrada. Bantam Books, 1540 Broadway, New York, New York 10036.*

PRINTED IN THE UNITED STATES OF AMERICA

OPM        0 9 8 7 6 5 4 3 2 1

# CHAPTER 1

# Dream Vacation

"**O**w!" I yelled, rubbing my arm. "Why did you pinch me?" I asked Jessica.

"I wanted to make sure I wasn't dreaming," Jessica said.

"Then you should have asked me to pinch *you*," I told her.

"But that would have hurt." Jessica made a face.

Jessica is so naughty sometimes! *I* would never pinch *her* without asking first. But I couldn't blame Jessica for feeling as if she were dreaming. Our family—plus my brother Steven's friend Joe—was about to start a vacation at the biggest and best amusement park in the world: Fantasy Forest. Steven, Jessica, and I had been trying to talk our parents into taking us there practically forever.

And at that very moment, Mom and Dad were standing in line to buy our tickets. The rest of us were waiting for them next to a big shiny purple sign that read Welcome to Fantasy Forest.

By the way, my name's Elizabeth Wakefield. Jessica is my twin sister. We're both seven years old and we look exactly alike. That's because we're *identical* twins.

Jessica has blue-green eyes. So do I. And we both have long blond hair with bangs. When we wear clothes that match, nobody can tell who is Elizabeth and who is Jessica. It's funny! Sometimes we can even fool Mom and Dad and Steven.

Steven is two years older than me and Jessica. He thinks he's great. Jessica and I think he's a big pain.

But Jessica and I don't agree on everything. For example, I love school. I even like homework. My favorite subject is reading. That's because I want to be a writer when I grow up. But Jessica doesn't like the learning part of school. She likes recess and lunch and seeing her friends Lila Fowler and Ellen Riteman.

Sometimes people are surprised that Jessica and I are so different. They think we should be the same *inside* because we look the same on the *outside*. That's silly. Every person in the whole world is different inside.

But even though we like different things, Jessica and I are best friends. Jessica loves being a twin. So do I. Well, at least most of the time. See, Jessica has one bad habit. She's always getting me into trouble.

We'd gotten into *big* trouble while Mom and Dad were planning our vacation. It all started when Jessica and I heard that our favorite radio station was giving away a trip to Fantasy Forest. Jessica actually won! But there was one problem: We were

3

supposed to be thirteen to enter. Jessica talked me into trying to convince the man at the radio station we were old enough. But at the last second, I couldn't go through with it. I told the radio man the truth. And it's because we told the truth that our parents let us go to Fantasy Forest. We had wanted to come here ever since we were babies!

"What's taking Mom and Dad so long?" Steven asked.

I shrugged. "That line is awfully long."

"Maybe we'll get to spend our entire vacation waiting in line," Joe said. "Wouldn't *that* be fun?"

Jessica and I giggled.

Joe is Steven's best friend. Steven got to bring him along so that he would have a friend to hang out with at Fantasy Forest. Jessica and I didn't need to bring friends— we had each other! Joe could be funny sometimes. But he could also be mean.

I watched all the people passing us.

But I didn't see Mom and Dad.

"We can't forget to go to the Princess Pageant," Jessica told me. "It only plays once while we're here. This afternoon at five."

"I know, I know," I said. Jessica had reminded me about the Princess Pageant about a hundred times already.

The Princess Pageant is a special show where dresses that belonged to real-life princesses are modeled. I'm not that interested in princess dresses. But seeing the pageant was one of the things Jessica was most excited to do at Fantasy Forest.

"Here come Mom and Dad!" Steven yelled.

"I see them!" Jessica said, jumping up and down.

Mom and Dad hurried toward us. "OK, kids, we're all set," Dad announced.

"Listen up," Mom said. She held up six bright yellow cards on thin chains. "These are our passes—one for each of us. You'll need to show them before you get on any of the rides. Hang them around your neck and be sure not to lose them."

Jessica and I put on our passes. We traded happy smiles.

"Everyone ready?" Dad asked. We nodded. "Then let's go!" he said.

The entrance to the park was like nothing I had ever seen. There was a big shiny gate that looked like it was made out of gold. I was looking up so much, I almost bumped into Steven.

"Hey, watch where you're going, squirt," he said. We showed our passes to a guard who was standing near the entrance. Then Dad led us through a passage that was made with hedges shaped like rabbits and giraffes! Fantasy Forest's main street is called Robin Hood Road. It's crammed full of cool toy stores and clothing shops. And there are lots of fast-food stands selling neat stuff like giant lollipops and strawberry shakes.

"Wow," Jessica said. Her eyes were open wide.

Tons of people were walking around, eating and talking and laughing. Fantasy Forest workers in green outfits were giving directions and making sure no little kids got lost. In the distance, we could see roller-coaster tracks, and the Ferris wheel spinning high above the trees. And I could even see the towers of a beautiful castle.

"Look, Jessica—the Enchanted Castle!" I shouted.

"Let's go there first!" Jessica squealed.

Steven and Joe traded disgusted looks.

"Forget it, shrimps," Steven said. "I'm not wasting my time in some baby castle. I want to ride the Screaming Squall first." The Screaming Squall is the biggest roller coaster at Fantasy Forest. Steven had been talking about riding it for weeks.

Joe nodded. "I vote for the Screaming Squall too."

"I want the Enchanted Castle!" Jessica said, putting her hands on her hips.

"Screaming Squall!" Steven screamed.

"Kids!" Mom exclaimed. "What's the

problem? We've only been here five minutes and you're already fighting!"

"The twins want to go in some stupid baby castle!" Steven made it sound as if it were the dumbest thing he'd ever heard.

"Why is that such a big deal?" Dad asked.

"Because Joe and I don't want to waste our time!" Steven said. "Being stuck with a couple of seven-year-olds is going to ruin my vacation."

Mom and Dad looked at each other. I felt sorry for them. They were on vacation too. And Steven was acting like a brat.

Jessica poked me in the side. "Steven is such a pain sometimes!"

I couldn't have agreed more.

# CHAPTER 2

# The Enchanted Castle

"What do you girls want to do first?" Mom asked.

"Visit the Enchanted Castle," Jessica said.

"And ride the Ferris wheel and the bumper cars," I added.

"And we want to see the Princess Pageant," Jessica put in.

"I already know about that," Mom said with a smile. Jessica had been reminding Mom about the pageant too.

Mom turned to Steven and Joe. "What do you boys want to ride?"

"The Screaming Squall," Steven said.

"Fantasy Forest has six big roller

coasters," Joe said. "I want to try all of them at least ten times!"

"How about if we take turns choosing rides?" Mom suggested. "Then everyone will get a chance to try the ones they want."

Jessica stuck out her lower lip. "But Elizabeth and I can't even ride the Screaming Squall," she whined. "We're too short."

"How do you know?" Dad asked.

"Lila was here last month and she was too short," Jessica reported. "And Lila is at least an inch taller than me."

Lila Fowler is Jessica's best friend at school. She's the one who had told Jessica about the Princess Pageant.

"Hmm," Mom said. "I guess that does change things. Making you girls wait in line for a ride you can't even get on doesn't seem fair."

"Making us wait for baby stuff isn't fair either!" Steven added.

Jessica rolled her eyes.

I shook my head. Steven was acting like

we are little kids. Which is silly. Jessica and I are very grown-up. Ask anyone.

Mom and Dad whispered together for a few seconds.

Then Dad gave us a wink. "Since both groups want to do different things, we think it's OK if we split up," he announced. "After all, Fantasy Forest is supposed to be the safest amusement park around. Steven and Joe, you can explore the park by yourself."

"Us too?" Jessica demanded.

"Yes," Mom said.

Jessica shot me a surprised look. She hadn't been expecting that answer. Neither had I.

"All right!" I exclaimed.

"Thanks, Mom and Dad!" Steven said. He gave Joe a high five.

"There are some rules, though," Mom told us. "We want you to stick together in pairs. If you have any trouble, ask a Fantasy Forest worker for help. And you have to check in with us for meals."

"No problem!" Jessica said. Steven, Joe, and I agreed. Dad told us to meet for lunch at noon at the Pie-in-the-Sky Pizza Parlor.

"Your dad and I are going to buy some souvenirs for everyone back home. We'll see you at noon at the pizza parlor. Have fun!" Mom said. She gave Jessica and me each a hug.

Jessica grabbed my hand. "Come on," she said. "Let's go see the Enchanted Castle."

We took off down Robin Hood Road. The pathways twisted and turned. A few minutes later, we were there.

Jessica drew in her breath. "It's *so* beautiful!"

I nodded. The castle was made of white glittery stone. Six towers rose up against the sky. The castle looked like a drawing from one of our storybooks—a drawing of the castle where Cinderella and her prince live happily ever after. Only, this castle was real!

"Look how many people are waiting to

13

get in!" Jessica said. The line snaked around and around in big loops in front of the castle.

"Wow," I said. "Come on, let's get in line before anyone else gets in front of us."

Jessica and I ran to the end of the line.

"What does that sign say?" Jessica asked.

I stood on my tiptoes so I could see a colorful sign in front of us. "It says ONE HOUR FROM THIS POINT!" I told Jessica.

Jessica's eyes widened in horror. But then she shrugged. "Oh, who cares?" she said. "Seeing the castle will be worth it."

So Jessica and I started to wait. We watched the people strolling by. We looked at our map. After a few minutes, we shuffled forward a step or two. I started to get bored. I wished I had a book. Standing in that line started to make my feet hurt.

"Let's play a game," I suggested to help pass the time. "Pretend you live in the Enchanted Castle. Where would you have your bedroom?"

"In the highest tower," Jessica said immediately.

I wasn't so sure. Bad things always seemed to happen to people in high towers. Evil kings were always locking fair maidens up in them. I studied the castle's windows, trying to decide which room would make the best bedroom.

"Look!" I said with a gasp.

"What?" Jessica asked.

I pointed to one of the lower windows. "A man is looking out that window!"

"I don't see anything," Jessica said.

"He was right there!" I insisted.

"Sure," Jessica said, rolling her eyes. "It must have been the prince."

"I'm not kidding," I said. "I saw a man's face."

"You're imagining things," Jessica said.

But I felt a shiver run up my spine. Something mysterious was going on in the Enchanted Castle. I was sure of it!

# CHAPTER 3

# Secret Passes

"We're next," Jessica said.

The ride operator motioned for us to step forward. "Climb into this boat," she told us.

Jessica and I climbed into a beautiful gold-and-white boat. Then we were drifting into the castle.

"Ahh," Jessica breathed as we floated into the first room. We were looking at a scene from *Snow White*. The witch offered Snow White a yummy-looking apple. Snow White took a bite. Then she slumped down and closed her eyes. The witch laughed an evil laugh.

Jessica reached for my hand. "That was scary!"

Then we were drifting into a scene from *Cinderella*. The prince gave her a shiny glass slipper and it fit! Next came *Sleeping Beauty*. And then the story of *Rapunzel*. Each scene was more beautiful than the last.

"That was great," I said. "But it was over so *fast!*"

Jessica and I climbed out of the boat.

"Let's go again!" Jessica said.

"OK!" I agreed.

We ran for the end of the line.

"Which room was your favorite?" Jessica asked me as we started to wait.

"I like Cinderella best," said a boy around our age with light brown hair who was standing near us. He was wearing red shorts and a T-shirt. Around his neck hung a chain with a bright red pass.

"How come?" Jessica asked.

"Did you see all of the mirrors the stepsisters were looking into?" the boy asked.

18

"Yes," I said.

"Well, if you look in a certain one, you can see the prince standing in the doorway," the boy told us. "He's holding the glass slipper. But you can only see him in that reflection."

"That's cool!" I said.

"I didn't notice that," Jessica said with a frown.

"I didn't notice it at first either," the boy told her.

"How many times have you been on this ride?" I asked him.

The boy shrugged. "I lost count. By the way, I'm Billy."

Jessica and I told Billy our names.

"Where are your parents?" Billy asked us.

"They're letting us explore the park by ourselves." Jessica explained.

"Parents do that all the time," Billy told us. "But last week some kids never showed up to meet their mom and dad."

"Were they lost?" Jessica asked, wide-eyed.

19

"No," Billy said with a giggle. "They were hiding! The guards found them under a table in the Nuthin' but Candy shop. They wanted to spend another day in the park."

Jessica smiled. "I don't blame them!"

I was surprised Jessica was being so nice to Billy. She doesn't usually like boys. But I was glad Jessica was being nice. I liked Billy.

"How did you hear about those kids?" I asked him.

Billy shrugged. "My dad told me."

"I can't believe your parents let you go around all by yourself," I said to Billy. "Our mom and dad made us promise to stay in pairs."

"Well, actually they . . . ," Billy said. "Hey, do you guys want to know a secret?"

"All right," I said.

"Do you promise not to tell anyone?" Billy asked. "Especially not any grown-ups?"

"OK," Jessica said right away.

"Well . . ." I hate secrets with rules. But I was curious. "OK," I said slowly.

Billy pulled two bright red Fantasy Forest passes out of his pocket. They looked just like his.

"Put these on," Billy said.

"Why?" Jessica asked.

"So I can show you the secret," Billy said.

Jessica and I traded puzzled looks. Then Jessica shrugged and slipped the red pass around her neck. I did the same with mine.

Billy looked pleased. "Follow me!" He stepped out of line and started to make his way back toward the end.

"Where is he going?" I wondered out loud.

"I don't know," Jessica said with a frown. "But if we follow him, we're going to lose our place."

The line stretched out a long way behind us.

"What should we do?" I asked Jessica.

Billy waved for us to follow him.

"Don't worry about the line!" he yelled.

"Let's go," Jessica said. "I want to know what the secret is. We can always get back in line later."

"Well, OK," I agreed.

Jessica and I ran after Billy.

"Come on," he said, leading us around the side of the ride.

As I hurried after Billy and Jessica, I noticed a bald, tough-looking man a few feet away, watching us. He looked just like the man I'd seen in the window of the Enchanted Castle! He didn't look like a dad on vacation. He was wearing dark pants and a dark shirt. And he didn't look like he was having fun.

"Hey, you guys, wait up!" I called after Jessica and Billy. I ran to catch up with them. And when I glanced over my shoulder, the man was gone.

Billy opened a gate with a sign on it that read Staff Only.

"Where are we going?" Jessica demanded.

"You'll see," Billy said.

"I don't want to get in trouble," I told him.

"You won't," Billy said. "I promise."

Billy stepped inside the gate. Jessica and I followed. One of the ride operators was standing just inside. But she didn't look mad. Instead, she took a quick look at our red passes and opened another gate for us. We went through—and came out right in the front of the line! Another ride operator waved us into a boat. Seconds later, we were gliding into the Enchanted Castle!

# CHAPTER 4

# Ferris-wheel Fun

"That was so cool!" Jessica said as we got off the Enchanted Castle ride for the second time.

"How come the ride operator let us in like that?" I asked Billy.

"It's the red passes," Billy explained.

"They must be expensive!" Jessica said.

Billy shook his head. "You can't buy them."

"So where did you get them?" I asked.

"That's a secret," Billy said.

*Did Billy steal the passes?* I wondered. *If he did, we have to give them back.* I bit my lip, trying to decide what to do. I didn't want to hurt Billy's feelings by asking if he was a thief. And something told me he *wasn't*. He seemed too nice. Still, something strange was going on.

"What else can the passes do?" Jessica asked Billy.

"I'll show you," Billy offered. "What ride do you want to go on next?"

"How about the Ferris wheel?" Jessica asked.

Billy looked at me.

"OK," I agreed. I decided I would ask Billy about the passes later.

"Come on, then!" Billy led us to the Ferris wheel. It was the biggest Ferris wheel I'd ever seen. It was higher than all the trees and almost as high as the Enchanted Castle! Again, we went through a gate marked Staff Only and came out right in the front of the line. We climbed into a bright red car. It was big enough for four people.

The ride operator pointed to a girl with pigtails who was at the front of the line. Standing next to her was a little girl who was around five years old. "There's room for you in this car with these kids," he said to Pigtails. He pointed to Jessica, Billy, and me.

Pigtails crossed her arms in front of her chest. "I want a car of my own."

"Unless nobody else is in line, I can't give you a car of your own," the ride operator told her. "Now, this is the last space on this ride. If you don't get on, you'll have to wait until the next one."

Pigtails stuck her nose in the air. "I'll wait," she said. "I want a car of my own."

The ride operator sighed. "OK, then, you're up!" he said to the next person in line—the little five-year-old girl.

The little girl shook her head. "I want to go with my sister," she said. "I'm scared."

"Tough," Pigtails replied. "I'm getting a car of my own. And no whiny babies are allowed in it." She gave the little girl a shove toward our car.

The little girl slowly climbed in. Her

lower lip was quivering, and she was taking quick little breaths. I always do that myself when I'm trying to keep from crying.

Jessica and I looked at each other. We thought Steven was bad. But Pigtails was twice as mean!

"I'm glad you decided to ride with us," Billy told the little girl, who sat down next to him. "And don't worry. This ride is lots of fun. It's not scary at all."

"Thanks," the little girl whispered. She gave Billy a shaky smile. Then she told us her name was Annie.

"Are you having fun at Fantasy Forest?" Billy asked Annie.

"Not really," Annie said with a sigh.

"Why not?" I asked her.

"My sister won't go on any of the rides with me," Annie said sadly. "I feel like I'm here all alone."

When Billy heard that, he looked really angry.

The ride started.

"Wow!" Jessica said as our car climbed

higher. "We can see the entire park!"

"The people on the ground look so small!" Annie exclaimed.

"We can see the tops of everyone's heads!" I added.

Jessica and Annie giggled. But Billy was still frowning. The angry look didn't leave his face for the whole ride—even though Annie seemed to be having a good time.

"Wait for me," Billy whispered to me and Jessica as we got off the ride. "I have to do something."

Jessica, Annie, and I watched as Billy walked up to the ride operator. They whispered back and forth. Then Billy ran over to us. "Watch what happens next!" he said.

Pigtails got on the ride. The operator let her have her own car on the ride, just like she wanted. When all the cars were full, the Ferris wheel started up again. But when Pigtails was at the very top, the ride jerked to a stop.

Jessica gasped.

"What's wrong?" Annie asked.

"Nothing," Billy told her. "It's just a joke. But don't tell your sister that."

Minutes passed, but the ride didn't start again. Pigtails was way at the top. Her car swung squeakily back and forth way up high above the park. I was glad I wasn't stuck up there all alone.

"What's wrong with the ride?" Pigtails shrieked loudly enough for everyone to hear. The ride operator didn't answer.

"Please start the ride!" Pigtails shouted, sounding like she was about to cry. "I'm scared! Get me down from here!"

The ride operator looked at Billy.

Billy nodded.

The ride operator winked at Billy and started up the Ferris wheel. A few minutes later, Pigtails got off the ride and ran right to Annie. Her eyes were opened really wide, and she was shaking a little. She didn't look so tough anymore.

"Are you OK?" Annie asked her sister.

"I guess so," Pigtails said, trying to

catch her breath. "But it was scary up there by myself."

"I know," Annie said. "I've been going on lots of rides alone. Now you know how I feel."

"I'm sorry, Annie," Pigtails said softly. "We can go on rides together from now on. What should we go on next?"

"Rocket to the Stars!" Annie said right away.

Pigtails looked surprised. "That ride's supposed to be pretty scary."

"Don't worry," Annie told her. "I'll hold your hand."

Pigtails looked kind of embarrassed. "OK, it's a deal," she said.

Annie and Pigtails walked off together. Then Annie remembered us. She turned around and waved.

"That was great!" Jessica said as we waved back. "That girl got just what she deserved."

I agreed. And it made me happy to think Pigtails would be nicer to Annie.

But something was bothering me.

"How did you get the Ferris wheel man to do that?" I asked Billy.

Billy just smiled. "Do you guys want to play some games now?"

What I really wanted was some *answers*. But Jessica was already following Billy to the arcade. I sighed and followed them.

# CHAPTER 5

# Double Prizes—for Free!

"Do you like to play arcade games?" Billy asked me.

I shrugged. I was feeling grumpy because Billy wouldn't tell me where he had gotten the red passes. Or how he had gotten the Ferris wheel operator to stop the ride.

"Elizabeth loves the softball toss," Jessica told him.

"Me too!" Billy said. "Come on, I'll show you where the Chipmunk's Nest Arcade is. It's pretty cool!"

The arcade was crowded with dozens of games. But Billy knew just where he was going. He led us right up to the softball toss.

"Good morning, kids," the man running the softball toss greeted us. Behind him were stacks of old-fashioned milk bottles in bright colors. And hanging above his head were hundreds of cool stuffed animals.

"Who would like to play?" the man asked with a grin.

"She would," Billy said, nodding at me.

The man handed me three light blue softballs. I started to pull a dollar bill out of my pocket.

"Keep your money!" the man said.

"Why?" I asked, surprised.

The man pointed to the red pass hanging around my neck. "That makes the game free."

My jaw dropped. "Really?"

"Really," the man said.

"Cool!" Jessica said.

I threw my three softballs. The first two missed the milk bottles completely. With the third one, I knocked down one bottle.

"Not bad," the man said, placing the

softballs in front of me. "Try again."

"Are you sure it's OK?" I asked. I felt funny playing without paying.

"I'm sure," the man said.

So I played again. That time I didn't knock down *any* bottles. But on my next turn, I knocked down an entire stack.

Jessica clapped for me. "That was great, Lizzie!"

"Try again!" Billy said.

"OK!" I said. I was having fun. I had played the softball toss before. But I usually had to stop after a few tries. Since the game was free, I could play as long as I wanted!

I took the first ball, aimed, and threw it carefully. Bam! One stack of bottles fell.

"Do it again," Jessica said.

I threw the second ball. Another stack of bottles hit the ground.

"Yippee!" Billy said. "One more stack and you win a prize!"

"Really?" I said.

The man nodded. "Your choice of any of the stuffed animals."

Jessica tilted her head upward. "Wow," she said. "Come on, Lizzie! You can do it again."

My hands felt sweaty. I wiped them on my shorts and then picked up the last ball. Then I took a deep breath. I closed my eyes and threw the ball as hard as I could.

Billy patted me on the back. "Way to go!" he said.

I opened one eye. I'd knocked down another stack of bottles!

"You win!" the man told me.

"Can I help you pick your stuffed animal?" Jessica asked.

"Sure," I said.

"Let's get that bright pink flamingo," Jessica suggested.

I wrinkled my nose. Real flamingos are beautiful. But the stuffed one Jessica was pointing at was too *pink*.

"How about the dinosaur instead?" I asked.

Jessica put her hands on her hips. "We already have *two* stuffed dinosaurs."

"If we had three, they could have adventures together," I said.

The man behind the counter started to laugh. "For twins, you sure do have a hard time agreeing. But don't worry. You can each choose a stuffed animal."

I gave the man a surprised look. "How come?"

"Any friend of Billy's gets double prizes," the man said.

"Great!" Jessica said. "I want the flamingo!"

The man got it down for her.

"Thanks!" Jessica said with a broad smile.

"And how about you?" the man asked me. "What would you like?"

"Um—the dinosaur, please," I told him.

The man got the dinosaur down and handed it to me. "There you go!"

"Thanks," I said uncomfortably. I felt funny taking the stuffed animal. After all, I hadn't paid to play the game. Getting double prizes just didn't seem right.

"What do you want to play now?" Billy asked as we walked away from the softball toss.

"I'm not sure," I said slowly. "Billy— how did that man know your name?"

Billy's face turned red. "Well—"

Just then I saw the scary man I'd seen earlier in the day. He was sitting on a bench near the Acorn Tree House. Was he following us? I nudged Jessica, but she was too busy looking at her new flamingo. Then I saw a big clock on top of a stand selling cotton candy. It said 12:05.

"Oh my gosh, Jessica!" I yelled. "We're five minutes late to meet Mom and Dad!"

She gasped. "We'd better get going!"

But we had no idea how to get back to the restaurant where we were supposed to meet Steven, Joe, and our parents!

# CHAPTER 6
# Muscle Man

"Where are you supposed to meet your family?" Billy asked.

"At the Pie-in-the-Sky Pizza Parlor on Robin Hood Road," Jessica told him.

"Don't worry," Billy said. "I know a shortcut."

Billy started to hurry through the crowd. Jessica and I followed him down twisting streets and past fun-looking rides we hadn't had time to try yet. A few minutes later, we were in front of the Pie-in-the-Sky Pizza Parlor. I was surprised by how well Billy knew his way around Fantasy Forest. How many days had he been here?

"Can we meet you after lunch?" Jessica asked Billy.

"Sure," Billy said. "But, um, I think you guys better give me back your red passes until then. Remember, they're a secret."

Jessica and I shared a look. I could tell Jessica didn't want to turn over her pass. But when I pulled mine over my head, she did the same.

Billy smiled at us. "Meet me by the Sawmill Splash on Lion Lane, when you're finished eating. I'll give you the passes back then."

"OK," Jessica said, and I nodded.

"Remember, don't tell anyone about the passes," Billy said.

"We won't," I told him.

Billy gave us a little wave and then started off toward the Ferris wheel.

"Come on," Jessica said. "Let's go inside. I'm hungry!"

I was about to follow Jessica into the restaurant when I saw that scary man again. He was looking right at me. My heart started to pound.

"Jessica, look at that man!" I whispered.

Jessica turned to where I was pointing. "He's tall."

"Much taller than Dad," I said with a nod. "And he looks strong. See how big his muscles are?"

"So what?" Jessica asked.

The man started to walk toward the Ferris wheel—in the same direction Billy had gone. I grabbed Jessica's arm. "That's the man I saw in the window of the Enchanted Castle. And I saw him again when we were by the softball toss!" I bit my lip. "The muscle man is following Billy!" I exclaimed.

Jessica looked at me like I was crazy. "Maybe he just wants to ride the Ferris wheel."

"He hasn't been on any rides all day," I said.

"How do you know?" Jessica demanded.

"Because I've seen him a bunch of

times already. He just stands and watches us," I told her. "I think something strange is going on with Billy."

"And I think you're so hungry that you're seeing things," Jessica said. "I'd better get you inside *fast*."

I giggled. Maybe Jessica was right. I *do* have an active imagination sometimes. And I *was* awfully hungry.

Jessica and I went inside the restaurant. Mom and Dad were sitting at a big round table that looked like a giant pizza. They were all alone. They looked relieved when they saw us walk in.

"Hi!" Jessica said as we sat down.

"You're fifteen minutes late!" Mom said, squeezing our hands.

"We're sorry," I said.

"Did you get lost?" Dad asked. He passed around glasses filled with soda.

"A little," I admitted. "But Billy showed us the way."

"Who's Billy?" Mom asked.

Jessica's eyes were round. She shook

her head at me. I knew she was trying to remind me not to mention the red passes. But Billy hadn't said we couldn't mention *him*.

"A boy we met," I said calmly. "We went on some rides with him."

"That's nice. . . ." Mom sounded as if she wasn't really paying attention. "Did you girls see Steven and Joe?" The restaurant was filling up with people fast.

"No," Jessica said. She took a slice of the large pizza Mom and Dad had ordered.

"I wonder where they could be," Mom said, glancing toward the door.

Jessica and I looked at each other. Mom sounded worried.

"So did you girls have a good time this morning?" Dad asked.

Jessica nodded her head eagerly. "It was great! We—"

"Here come the boys!" Mom interrupted.

I looked up and saw Steven and Joe come in.

"Where have you been?" Mom asked them when they got to the table. "You're almost twenty minutes late!"

"Sorry," Steven said. "We *just* got off the Screaming Squall. To get here on time, we would have had to get out of line right when we were at the front."

"Maybe that's what you should have done," Dad said sternly.

Steven looked horrified. "But we waited in that line all morning!"

"*All* morning?" Jessica repeated.

Joe nodded as he slid into a seat. "For two hours and forty-six minutes," Joe said. He has a stopwatch on his watch.

"But it was worth it," Steven said. "The Screaming Squall was awesome!"

Jessica shook her head. "Still, you guys just rode one ride all morning! Elizabeth and I did lots more than that. We went in the Enchanted Castle—"

"Twice!" I put in.

"Twice," Jessica said with a nod. "And we went on the Ferris wheel, and then

Elizabeth won these stuffed animals in the arcade." She held up the flamingo and the dinosaur.

"You two really *did* do a lot," Mom said.

"Big deal," Steven said with a frown.

"Who wants to go on those baby rides, anyway?" Joe asked.

"Not me," Steven replied. "I'd rather wait in line all day than spend time with a couple of seven-year olds."

Jessica and I smiled secretly to each other. Steven and Joe thought they were so great!

"Now remember, we're going to meet at six o'clock at Chipmunk Cavern, OK?" Mom said. "Now, you know where it is?"

"Yeah, yeah," Steven said. "Right on Tree Gnome Lane."

"Six o'clock sharp," Dad said sternly. "We don't want you kids to be late like last time."

"OK," I said. "We promise we'll be there at six o'clock exactly." I looked at Jessica to agree with me, but she had already started walking down Robin Hood Road.

# CHAPTER 7

# Steven and Joe's Bumpy Ride

"There's Billy!" Jessica said. He was waiting for us in front of the Sawmill Splash, just like he said he would.

I looked around for the muscle man. And there he was! He was kind of hiding behind a big wooden statue of a hedgehog, just across from the Sawmill Splash. He watched as Jessica ran over to say hi to Billy.

I hurried over to join them. "Billy, I have to tell you something important. There's a man—"

"Here are your red passes," Billy interrupted.

"Thanks!" Jessica grabbed one of them and slipped it around her neck.

"But *Billy*," I said.

Jessica gave me an impatient look. "Please stop worrying about that man," she whispered to me.

I took the other red pass from Billy. But I didn't put it on right away. I felt funny taking it. Where did he get the red passes, anyway? And why didn't he want us to tell anyone about them? And where were his parents? I was sure that something strange was going on with Billy. He had too many secrets. And even though Jessica thought I was crazy, I was *sure* the muscle man was following him.

"Should we go on the Sawmill Splash?" Jessica asked Billy.

"It's fun," Billy told her. "As long as you don't mind getting wet!"

Jessica wrinkled her nose. "I don't want to get *really* wet."

"Then you should sit in one of the backseats," Billy told her. "You'll stay driest there."

"Cool," Jessica said. "Let's go!"

"Come on, Elizabeth!" Billy said.

Part of me felt like I shouldn't go. But the Sawmill Splash really *did* look like fun. And the line to get on *was* awfully long. Finally, I sighed and put the red pass around my neck. I couldn't help myself. The red pass made Fantasy Forest even more fun. And so did hanging out with Billy.

We went right to the front of the line. Billy and I climbed into a boat that looked as if it had been cut out of a huge log. Jessica sat in the seat behind us. The boats didn't have rails under them like roller coasters do, just large tubes of water. We started to move. Our boat climbed to the top of a really high hill and then it zipped through tunnels so fast that we were leaning to the side and getting splashed a little. Then our boat climbed an even bigger hill and suddenly swooshed down really fast into a big pool of water! Billy and I got soaking wet, but

Jessica stayed pretty dry, just like Billy said she would. By the time we got off the ride, we were all smiling and laughing.

"That was fun!" Jessica said. "And I didn't even get my sundress wet!" Billy and I laughed.

"What do you want to go on next?" Billy asked as we walked away from the Sawmill Splash.

I looked around to see what was nearby. "How about the bumper cars?" By that time, I was having too much fun to worry about the muscle man.

"OK," Billy agreed.

Jessica nodded.

"Choose a car on the outside," Billy told us as we walked around the line. "Sometimes the people on the inside get stuck there."

"Uh-oh," Jessica whispered.

"What's the matter?" Billy asked her.

"Steven and Joe are in this line," Jessica whispered.

"Who?" Billy asked.

"Our brother and his friend," I explained.

"We can't let them see your red passes," Billy whispered. "Come on."

Billy led us through a gate that said Staff Only. But this gate didn't lead us to the front of the line. It opened onto a staircase that led up onto a balcony above the bumper cars. Below us, we could see the cars zipping around bumping each other. We could also see the line of people waiting to get on the bumper cars.

"There's Steven and Joe," Jessica said, pointing them out to Billy. They were getting close to the front of the ride.

"They look nice," Billy said.

Jessica rolled her eyes. "They're *not*."

"They keep saying the rides we like are for babies," I explained. "Steven said his day would be ruined if they had to spend it with us."

"Sounds like Pigtails," Billy said.

Jessica grinned. "I wish we could show Steven and Joe just like we showed her," she said.

"We can!" Billy said. "Stay here."

Billy ran down the stairs. From our spot on the balcony, Jessica and I saw Billy appear at the front of the line. He whispered something to the ride operator. A minute later, Billy was back standing next to us.

"What's going on?" I asked Billy.

Billy studied the line. "Steven and Joe should get on the next ride. You'll see then."

A few seconds later, the cars came to a stop. The people who had been riding in them undid their seat belts and got out. When all of those people were gone, the ride operator opened the gate. New people flooded into the bumper cars. Steven and Joe were some of the first people in. They each ran for their own car.

"Now watch," Billy whispered.

The ride operator started walking from car to car. He checked to make sure that everyone was wearing their seat belts. When he got to Steven's car, he reached down and fiddled with something along the side. From where he was sitting, Steven couldn't see what was happening. Next, the ride operator did the same thing with Joe's car.

"What did the ride operator do?" Jessica asked.

"He turned off the switch that connects their cars to the power," Billy explained.

"You mean he unplugged their cars?" I asked.

"Right," Billy said.

"Why?" Jessica asked.

"You'll see," Billy told us.

The ride operator went back to his booth. He turned the ride on. Everyone started to zip around in their cars. That is, everyone except Steven and Joe.

A teenage girl bumped Steven's car—hard.

Steven gave the girl an angry look. He stomped his gas pedal with all of his might. But the car didn't move.

The teenager bumped Steven again.

We could hear the girl laughing.

Meanwhile, Joe was moving back and forth in his seat. Maybe he thought that would get his car moving. But it didn't.

"They don't know what's happening," Jessica said with a giggle.

Some of the other drivers noticed that Steven and Joe weren't moving—and they attacked! *Everyone* on the ride started bumping them. But Steven and Joe couldn't bump back.

"Stop hitting me!" Steven shouted at another driver.

"Yeah, cut it out!" Joe whined.

"This is great!" Jessica said, laughing. She held her hand in the air and I slapped her a high five. Steven and Joe didn't look—or sound—so grown-up now!

"Let's go walk by them!" Jessica said. "And let them know we saw the whole thing!"

"Yeah!" I said.

We climbed down from the balcony

and walked right by Steven and Joe, who were still stuck in the middle of the bumper cars.

"Having a little trouble with your cars?" Jessica asked.

"These darn cars won't work!" Joe yelled. "What's wrong with them?"

"Maybe you just don't know how to drive them," I said, and we all laughed. The look on Steven's and Joe's faces was worth the whole trip!

# CHAPTER 8

# Overboard!

"What should we ride next?" Billy asked.

We'd already tried the bumper cars, the haunted house, the fun house, the Spider, and a couple of roller coasters.

"I'm not sure," I said. "I can never make up my mind when I'm hungry."

"You're hungry?" Billy asked. "Let's get something to eat."

"I want some of those curly french fries," I told him.

Billy led us to a nearby stand. "Three orders of french fries," he said.

Jessica looked in her bag for money.

"You don't need that," Billy said.

"Why not?" Jessica asked.

"Red passes," Billy said with a grin.

Jessica and I shook our heads. The red passes were great! We carried our french fries over to a nearby picnic bench.

"What time is it?" Jessica asked as we started to eat.

"Four-thirty," Billy said.

"Four-thirty!" Jessica bounced up and down in her seat. "The Princess Pageant starts soon!"

"Why don't you come with us?" I asked him.

"I can't," Billy said.

"But you can't miss the Princess Pageant!" Jessica told him. "This is the only time it's playing this weekend."

Billy popped a french fry into his mouth. He was looking off into the distance.

I followed his gaze with my eyes. And guess what I saw? The scary muscle man! He was sitting on a bench and he was watching us! Billy looked at the muscle man and turned away really fast.

I put down the french fry I was holding. Suddenly I wasn't very hungry anymore.

"If you really want me to go with you, there is one way," Billy said. "Come on!"

Billy got up and started to hurry away from the bench. Jessica and I looked at each other with surprise. But then Jessica got up and rushed after Billy. I had to run to catch up with them.

"In here!" Billy said, pointing to the Pirates of the Pacific ride.

"What's going on?" I demanded.

"Just come on!" Billy hurried through the gate.

Jessica and Billy were waiting for me as I rushed up to the boat. As soon as they saw me coming, they jumped on. So did I.

The boat drifted away from the entrance. Billy looked over his shoulder and groaned. I looked too. The muscle man was in the boat behind us! *How did he get around the line?* I wondered. But then I saw a red pass hanging around his neck!

Then I thought I might know why the muscle man was following us. Maybe Billy had stolen the red passes from him. And now the muscle man was trying to get them back.

"Billy," I said. "That man is following us, isn't he?"

"Not for long," Billy said. "Come on!"

"We're in the middle of the ride!" Jessica said. "Where can we go?"

"Overboard!" Billy announced. He unbuckled his seat belt. Then he stood up, scrambled out of the boat, and jumped up on the bank.

The boat was still moving.

"Come on," Billy called. "You have to jump before the boat moves away from the bank!"

"Don't!" I yelled as Jessica undid her seat belt.

But before I could stop her, Jessica jumped out after Billy!

# CHAPTER 9

# Billy Gets Caught!

Jessica landed safely on the bank. "Come on, Elizabeth!" she yelled.

"You can do it!" Billy called. He was hurrying along the bank so that he stayed level with my boat.

I was mad! Jessica has gotten me in lots of sticky situations. But this one was definitely the worst.

"Mommy, Mommy, look where they are!" the little boy in the boat in front of me yelled. His mother turned around to look. When she saw Jessica and Billy standing on the bank, she grabbed the little boy's arm.

"Those children are very bad," the woman said.

*She's right,* I thought.

I looked behind me. The muscle man was standing up halfway in his boat—as if he was thinking about going after Billy and Jessica too.

All this time, my boat was moving forward. I only had another few seconds to decide what to do. Finally, I unbuckled my seat belt and stood up.

"Jump, Elizabeth!" Billy held out his hand to me. I grabbed it and jumped, landing on the bank just as my boat pulled away into the river. As I fell back on the bank, I looked up and saw the muscle man, who was floating past me in his boat. He looked furious.

The muscle man stood all the way up. His boat swayed back and forth. Then he jumped!

I scrambled to my feet. "He's going to get us!" I yelled to Billy.

But the muscle man's foot got caught on the side of his boat. *Kur-splash!* He fell in the water! When he came up for air, he looked even angrier than before.

"Run, you guys!" Jessica yelled. "Run!"

Billy grabbed my hand and pulled me toward a gray-bearded pirate.

I gasped. Until then, I'd been busy worrying about the muscle man. I'd forgotten about the pirates. I was sure this pirate would try to stop us. And then we'd get in trouble for getting off our boat.

But as Billy and I dashed past, the pirate just kept counting a big pile of money. After we passed him, I glanced back. That's when I discovered why the pirate wasn't interested in us. He wasn't real. I mean, I already knew he wasn't a real pirate. But he wasn't even a real person! From the back, you could see wires and cords coming out of him.

And the "island" the pirate was kneeling on turned out to be just scenery—like we used for the Thanksgiving play at school.

But the muscle man was real enough. And I knew it wouldn't be long before he climbed out of the water and came after us.

We ran up to a tall row of bushes.

"Now what?" Jessica asked. She was out of breath.

"Under the bushes!" Billy dropped to his hands and knees and started crawling.

Jessica made a face. But she got down and followed Billy. I followed Jessica. The branches scraped my back. I even had to crawl on my tummy for part of the way. I came out on a crowded pathway. People walking by stared at me. I was embarrassed.

But Billy smiled at me as I brushed off my shirt. "That was great! Butch will never get under those bushes!"

"Is Butch that big man with all the muscles?" I asked.

"Yes," Billy admitted.

"Why is he following you?" I asked.

"It's a long story," Billy said.

"We don't have time for a long story!" Jessica said. "The Princess Pageant is about to begin!"

"Then let's go!" Billy said. "It's this way."

"I'm not going anywhere until I find

out what's going on with the muscle man." I put my hands on my hips and planted my feet.

But Billy and Jessica didn't pay any attention. They rushed down the pathway without even glancing back.

*They are really starting to bug me,* I thought. But I didn't want to be left alone in the park. "Wait up, you guys!" I yelled and ran after them.

The three of us ran halfway across the park. When we got to the theater where the Princess Pageant was showing, it was mostly full. But Billy found us three seats together. As soon as we sat down, the lights started to dim. Jessica was bouncing with excitement. But I couldn't think about the show. I was too worried about Billy. He had told me the muscle man was following him. I was sure he was in trouble. Maybe we were too.

People started whispering and laughing behind us. I turned to see what was going on. The muscle man was coming down the aisle! His wet hair was sticking to his head. And his shoes were squeaking as he walked.

"Hide!" I whispered to Billy.

Billy tried to slip under his seat. But it was too late. The muscle man was standing right next to our row of seats!

# CHAPTER 10
## The Chase

The muscle man motioned for Billy to come out of the row of seats.

"Don't go," I whispered to him.

"I have to," Billy said in a sad voice. He stood up and slid toward the aisle. As soon as he got out, the muscle man took Billy's hand and marched him out of the theater.

"Let's go!" I said to Jessica, who hadn't seen Billy leave.

"Where are we going?" she asked.

"After Billy!" I said. "I think he's being kidnapped."

"Kidnapped . . . ," Jessica repeated. But I could tell she hadn't really heard me. She was staring at the stage. The

Princess Pageant was about to begin.

A second later Jessica snapped her head toward me. "Kidnapped?"

"Yes!" I said.

"But we'll miss the Princess Pageant!" Jessica said with a frown. She looked longingly at the stage, and then at my worried face. "All right," she said. "Let's go!"

We ran out of the theater. I searched the crowd outside for Billy.

"There they are!" Jessica yelled. She pointed to Billy and the muscle man. They were just passing the haunted house.

Jessica and I started to run after them. But it wasn't easy. The park was very crowded.

"Excuse me," I yelled as I ran.

"Coming through," Jessica called, side-stepping around a woman and a baby.

"Whoa!" I yelled, stopping short just before I ran into an elderly man.

"Slow down, Missy!" he told me.

"Sorry," I said.

But people kept getting in our way.

"I think we lost them," Jessica said.

I stood on my tiptoes and searched the crowd. "Look, there they are!"

Jessica saw them too. "They're heading for the Enchanted Castle," she said.

Jessica and I ran around the back side of the castle—away from where people were standing in line. We were just in time to see the muscle man and Billy disappear through a door. Jessica and I ran up to the door. I tried to turn the doorknob, but the door was locked.

"Why would they go into the castle?" I wondered out loud.

"Maybe this is the kidnapper's hideaway," Jessica suggested.

"Look!" I said, pointing to the castle wall. "There's a window."

"It's awfully high up," Jessica said.

"I think you can reach it if I lift you up," I said.

Jessica bit her lip. But then she nodded. "I'll do it for Billy," she said.

I knelt down so that Jessica could sit

on my shoulders. Then I slowly stood up. "Can you reach it?" I grunted.

"Easy!" Jessica said.

"Is it open?" I asked.

"Let me just try," Jessica said. "There! I got it!"

Jessica's weight lifted off my shoulders. I looked up and saw her feet disappearing into the window. Then Jessica popped her head out and held a hand down to me. I grabbed her hand and pulled myself up. I dropped down inside the castle window.

"Where are we?" I whispered, looking around in surprise.

"I don't know," Jessica admitted.

I was beginning to think climbing through the window wasn't a good idea. We'd been on the Enchanted Castle ride twice—and this definitely wasn't part of it. We were in a hallway that looked like part of someone's house. Light blue carpeting covered the floors, and there was flowered wallpaper on the walls.

71

"What should we do now?" Jessica whispered.

I looked at the door. Part of me wanted to sneak right back out. But then I thought about Billy. Wherever he was, he must be frightened.

"Let's find Billy," I whispered back. "Then we can get out of here."

Jessica nodded. All of the doors leading off the hallway were closed—except for one at the end. Jessica and I tiptoed up to the partly opened door and peeked into the room beyond. Inside were two desks. A fancy-looking computer and telephone sat on each one. Along one wall, television screens showed different views of the park.

"What are those screens for?" I wondered out loud.

"I don't know," Jessica whispered. "But it looks like something from a spy movie."

"Perfect for kidnappers," I whispered.

"Let's keep looking for Billy," Jessica whispered.

I nodded and followed Jessica back

down the hallway. We crept up a short flight of stairs.

Jessica stopped at the top of the stairs. "Look, there's a window here."

When I looked out the window, I could see a line of people waiting to get into the Enchanted Castle. I gasped. "Jessica, this must be the window I saw from the line this morning! I knew I had seen a face!"

"Shh!" Jessica whispered. "Do you hear that?"

I nodded. "Someone is crying!"

Jessica put her ear up to the first door in the hallway. "It's not coming from in there," she said, shaking her head.

I tiptoed to the next door and listened. "I think it's coming from in here," I whispered.

Jessica took a deep breath and slowly opened the door. We peeked into a bedroom that looked a lot like Steven's. Billy was lying facedown on the bed, sobbing.

"Don't cry, Billy." Jessica tiptoed up to the bed. "We came to rescue you."

Billy quickly sat up and turned to face us. His eyes were opened wide. "How did you get in here?"

"Don't worry about that," I whispered. "Just come on. We've got to get out of here!"

"Billy's not going anywhere," came a deep voice from behind us.

Jessica and I spun around. The muscle man was standing in the doorway. He was blocking the only way out. We were trapped!

# CHAPTER 11

# Inside the Castle

"You'd better let us go," Jessica told the muscle man fiercely. "All of us!"

The muscle man glanced at Jessica. Then he turned to Billy. "Are these girls bothering you?" he asked in a deep voice. His voice sounded concerned. I was confused. Why would Billy's kidnapper be nice to him?

"No," Billy told him. "They're my friends."

Billy turned to me and Jessica. "Sorry, but I think you guys better go. I'm in enough trouble already."

"I'll show you out," the muscle man said to me and Jessica.

"We know you're a kidnapper!" I

yelled. "We're not letting you get away with this!"

"He's not a kidnapper," Billy said, giggling. "He's my bodyguard."

I stared at Billy, completely shocked. "You mean you're not being kidnapped?"

Billy burst out laughing. "Of course not!"

Even the muscle man looked amused.

"But why do you need a bodyguard?" Jessica asked. "Are you a movie star?"

"No," Billy said. "I'm just a normal kid. But my family owns Fantasy Forest. We live here," he said.

Jessica's mouth hung open. So did mine. Neither of us could say a word. Then a man and a woman came into the room. The man was tall and friendly-looking, and the woman had the same color hair as Billy and was wearing a pretty linen dress.

"Billy! You know you're not supposed to have guests over. Who are these girls and what are they doing here?" the woman asked Billy sternly.

"I didn't know they were coming," Billy explained. "They just sort of . . . er, followed me home. Mom, Dad, this is Jessica and Elizabeth, my friends," he added politely. "Jessica and Elizabeth, these are my parents."

Jessica raised her eyebrows.

I knew what she was thinking. If Billy wasn't in trouble, maybe we were. It seemed like we had a lot of explaining to do.

"We're sorry," I told Billy's mom and dad. "See, we didn't know the muscle . . . um, Butch was Billy's bodyguard. When Butch led Billy away, we thought he was in trouble." I didn't mention that we had climbed in the window to find him.

Billy's mom's face softened. "You two came here just to make sure Billy was OK?"

I nodded.

"That was very sweet. I'm sorry if I was a little rude. You see, with us owning Fantasy Forest and Billy being our son, we feel very protective—"

"Too protective," Billy said. "I'm

never allowed to bring kids over, or go anywhere without Butch following me. "It's hard to make friends like a normal kid when I have to keep secrets."

"That's awful," Jessica said. I gave her a look. I didn't want her to be rude to Billy's parents.

Suddenly I looked past her to the giant fish clock on the wall. It was twenty past six. We were late to meet Mom and Dad again!

# CHAPTER 12

# Private Pageant

"We're already twenty minutes late to meet our parents," I explained, grabbing Jessica's hand.

"Mom and Dad will be mad!" Jessica said. "We'd better run!"

"Calm down, girls," Billy's dad said. "I'll go down to the office and call a guard near where you were supposed to meet your family. That way they'll know you're OK."

"We were supposed to meet them at Chipmunk Cavern," I said.

"OK. We'll tell the guard. Why don't we invite the girls' family to supper?" Billy's mom suggested. Our cook always fixes large meals in case we have guests."

Then she turned to me and Jessica. "That is, if you think that would be fun."

"Dinner in the Enchanted Castle?" Jessica said. "That sounds great!"

I nodded eagerly.

"Good!" Billy's mom winked at us and followed Billy's dad out of the room.

"See you later, buddy," Butch said. "Sorry about chasing you, and you girls too. I was just doing my job."

"That's OK," Billy said.

"Yeah, we didn't mind, Mr. Muscle Man, I mean Butch," Jessica said.

Butch smiled and left the room.

"I can't believe you get to have supper in the Enchanted Castle every day!" Jessica told Billy when we were alone.

"It's no big deal," Billy said.

"Maybe not to you," I said. "But we've never met anyone who lived in an amusement park before."

"That's because we're the only family in the world who does," Billy told me. "Most amusement parks are owned by big companies. But Mom and Dad own all of Fantasy Forest. And they like to be close to their work."

"That's so cool!" Jessica said. "Do you get to go on any ride you want whenever you want?"

"Sure," Billy said. "That's what the red passes are for."

"You mean your parents gave you the passes?" Jessica asked.

Billy nodded.

"Then why did we have to keep them secret?" I asked.

"Some people—mostly grown-ups—start acting weird when they find out Mom and Dad own the park," Billy explained. "They want to bring in all their friends for free. Or they want to ride the Screaming Squall all alone."

"I thought you had stolen the passes," I told Billy with a giggle. "I thought that was why Butch was following you."

Billy looked sad again. "Butch is *always* following me."

"Why do you need a bodyguard?" I asked.

Billy shrugged. "My parents just call Butch my bodyguard because they think I like it better. When I was a little kid, they called him my baby-sitter."

"I hate having baby-sitters," Jessica said.

"Me too!" Billy said forcefully.

"Maybe you should tell your parents you don't want to have a bodyguard anymore," I suggested.

"Maybe," Billy said sadly. "I don't know if my parents would listen. Besides, Butch and I are friends. I'd kind of miss him if he wasn't here anymore."

"Oh," I said. *Poor Billy,* I thought. *He has a big problem.*

Billy's mom poked her head into the room. "Girls, your family is here."

Jessica, Billy, and I walked down the stairs. Mom, Dad, Steven, and Joe were standing in front of the castle door with their eyes open wide.

"Cool!" Steven and Joe shouted.

"This is quite a place you've got here," my dad said to Billy's dad.

"Thanks. It's so nice to meet you. You have two wonderful girls," Billy's dad said. Jessica and I smiled. Steven made a face.

"Won't you all sit down for dinner?" Billy's mom asked, leading us into a huge dining room decorated all in lavender. We sat down at the table. Butch came in too.

"Were you worried when the girls didn't show up on time?" Billy's mom asked my mom as we ate delicious lasagne.

"Not *too* worried," Mom said. "We've heard that Fantasy Forest is one of the safest places in the world."

Billy's dad smiled broadly. "We work very hard to make sure our guests are never in the slightest bit of danger."

"Then why does Billy need a bodyguard?" I asked.

Butch's eyes opened wide.

Suddenly I was worried. I shouldn't have opened my big mouth.

Billy shot me a furious look. I covered

my mouth with my hand. I hadn't meant to say anything that might get Butch fired.

"So, did you have fun at the park today?" Billy's mom asked all of us.

"Definitely!" Jessica said, and I nodded.

Billy's mom turned to Steven and Joe. "How about you boys?"

"It was fun, I guess," Steven said carefully.

"You *guess?*" Dad repeated.

"Did something disappoint you?" Billy's mom asked.

"Something is wrong with the bumper cars," Steven said. "Our cars wouldn't move."

Jessica almost choked on her salad.

I had to bite my lip to keep from laughing out loud.

"We'll look into that," Billy's dad told Steven.

"Also, we had to wait in line for more than two hours to get on the Screaming Squall," Joe said.

"I'm sorry to hear that," Billy's dad

said. "The line there should move much more quickly. But Henry, the Screaming Squall's operator, isn't very good at keeping things moving."

"Henry used to run the Enchanted Castle," Billy's mom added. "And he did a beautiful job here."

"Too bad he's not *still* here," Jessica said. "The lines at the Enchanted Castle are superlong."

Suddenly, I had an idea. An absolutely beautiful idea. I crossed my fingers under the table and hoped that everything would happen the way I wanted.

"Maybe you should move Henry back to his job at the Enchanted Castle," I suggested.

Billy's mom looked at me. "That's a good idea. But then who could we get to operate the Screaming Squall?" she said. "We're terribly understaffed right now."

"Butch!" I exclaimed.

Everyone looked at me in surprise, including Butch. Suddenly I wasn't so sure my idea was a good one. But then Billy's eyes lit up and he smiled. I knew he understood what I was trying to do: get Butch a different job at Fantasy Forest.

"That's an interesting idea," Billy's dad told me kindly. "But Butch doesn't know anything about operating rides."

"Um . . . but he does know a lot about kids," I said.

"That's true," Billy agreed.

"And he's very patient," I went on. Butch smiled.

"Very!" Jessica said. "He waited around for us all day."

"Also, he's a tiny bit scary," I said. "Which would help him do a good job. Nobody in line would give him a hard time."

"How do you know Butch *wants* to run the Screaming Squall?" Billy's dad asked me.

"I don't," I admitted.

Everyone turned to look at Butch.

"I would like it very much," Butch said in his polite way. "I love roller coasters. That's why I came to work at Fantasy Forest in the first place. But I'm afraid I must say no. Billy needs me. And that's more important."

Billy's happy smile disappeared.

"Tell him the truth," I whispered to Billy.

Billy took a deep breath. "Actually . . ."

"Go on!" Jessica said.

"I don't want a bodyguard anymore," Billy said in a rush. "I think Butch would do a great job on the Screaming Squall. And we could still see each other every day."

"Then I'd be happy to accept the job," Butch said, grinning.

"Great!" Billy's dad said. "You can start your training tomorrow!"

Billy gave me a grateful look.

"I feel terrific," I whispered to Jessica. "I think everything is going to work out for Billy and Butch."

"I'm glad," Jessica said. But she didn't sound very happy.

"What's the matter?" I asked.

"I was just thinking about the Princess Pageant," Jessica admitted. "We're never going to see it now."

Billy's mom overheard this. "Well, we'll just have to bring the Princess Pageant to you," she said, and she hurried out of the room. Jessica and I couldn't believe our ears.

After our dessert of chocolate cake and strawberry ice cream, we had a private showing of the Princess Pageant! Twelve girls modeled dresses worn by famous princesses. Each one was more dazzling than the next.

"We have two more dresses and we don't have any more girls to wear them," Billy's mom said. "Any volunteers?"

Jessica practically jumped out of her seat. "I will!"

"Me too!" I exclaimed.

"These dresses were worn by two princess sisters who lived a long time ago in England," Billy's mom said as she helped

us put on our dresses in her bedroom.

"Wow, this really is an enchanted castle!" Jessica said.

My dress was light blue with sequins and lace. Jessica's was bright pink and made of shiny satin. We modeled them while everyone clapped and smiled. But Jessica and I were smiling the most. How's that for a fairy-tale ending?

*But Billy's family has one more gift to give to the Wakefields—a very big gift! Find out what it is in Sweet Valley Kids #68,* A ROLLER COASTER FOR THE TWINS!